Maddie's Big Test

Maddie's Big Test

Louise Leblanc

Illustrated by Marie-Louise Gay
Translated by Sarah Cummins

First Novels

Formac Publishing Company Limited
Halifax, Nova Scotia

Originally published as *Sophie est la honte de la famille*
Text copyright © 2006 Sarah Cummins
Illustration copyright © Marie-Louise Gay

Formac Publishing Company Limited recognizes the support of the
Province of Nova Scotia through the Department of Tourism, Culture and
Heritage. We acknowledge the financial support of the Government of
Canada through the Book Publishing Industry Development Program
(BPIDP) for our publishing activities.

Formac Publishing Company Limited acknowledges the support of the
Canada Council for the Arts for our publishing program.

NOVA SCOTIA
Tourism and Culture

The Canada Council | Le Conseil des Arts
for the Arts | du Canada

Library and Archives Canada Cataloguing in Publication
Leblanc, Louise, 1942-
[Sophie est la honte de la famille. English]
     Maddie's big test / Louise LeBlanc ; illustrations by
     Marie-Louise Gay ; translated by Sarah Cummins.

(First novels; 58)
Translation of: Sophie est la honte de la famille
ISBN-10: 0-88780-718-6 (bound) ISBN-13: 978-0-88780-718-3 (bound)
ISBN-10: 0-88780-714-3 (pbk.) ISBN-13: 978-0-88780-714-5 (pbk.)

     1. Maddie (Fictitious character : Leblanc)—Juvenile
fiction. 2. Academic achievement—Juvenile fiction.
     3. Cheating (Education)—Juvenile fiction.
     4. Schools—Juvenile fiction. I. Gay, Marie-Louise
     II. Cummins, Sarah III. Title. IV. Title: Sophie est
la honte de la famille.English. V. Series.

PS8573.E25S64313 2006   jC843'.54   C2006-904388-4

Formac Publishing Company Ltd.   Distributed in the United States by:
5502 Atlantic Street   Orca Book Publishers
Halifax, Nova Scotia, B3H 1G4   P.O. Box 468 Custer, WA
www.formac.ca   USA 98240-0468

Printed and bound in Canada

Table of Contents

To Pascale and Lorenzo,
my special advisors

1
No Need to Study

I am on pins and needles! I'm a contestant on *Road to Stardom* and the host is about to announce the results of the final vote.

"And the grand prize winner is … *Maddie*!"

The crowd leaps to their feet and cheers. What a triumph!

In the middle of all the screams and bravos, I hear a little *beep-beep*. What is that?

Grrr, it was my alarm clock. I turned it off and listened to the awful silence. Real life filled up all the space.

My problems suddenly took over.

For the last two days, I'd been shaking in my boots. Our report cards were due to arrive any day now, and my grades were rotten. My parents would die when they saw them. But wait! Maybe they hadn't picked up today's mail yet.

I jumped out of bed, pulled on my clothes, and rushed to the mailbox. It was full — hooray! I took out the package of stuff and rifled through it. No report card. What was going on? I wandered to the kitchen, perplexed.

"Well, if it isn't our new letter carrier!" said my mom.

What an idiot I am! I'd brought the mail with me.

"Is this what you were looking for?"

asked my dad, tossing my report card onto my plate.

I wished I could disappear under the table.

"I guess you've decided to repeat your grade," he said sternly.

"We'll be in the same class!" my brother Alexander snickered.

"Unless you have to repeat your grade!" My mom put him in his place.

"Neither one of you has any excuse," my dad said. "You're just lazy. You don't work hard enough."

"I study every night in my room!" I protested.

"You don't have good work habits," said my brother Julian.

What was he going on about, the little genius?

"You study in bed, listening to music. So you're lost in space — "

"With the stars!" my mother added.

"Tars!" screamed Angelbaby, splatting her pablum in the shape of a star.

She gurgled, proud of her new word. She won't be laughing when she has to study to learn new things!

"All you think about is that star show," my dad continued. "You're not being responsible, Maddie."

"I am so! I intend to win on *Road to Stardom* one day."

"In the meantime, you'd better put yourself on the road to school. You too, Alexander. Both of you!"

"All three," said my mom, with a funny look.

"All three?" My dad was puzzled.

"Julian's doing fine!"

"I was referring to myself," said my mother. "I'm going to finish my degree. I've already registered."

My dad was floored. And so were the rest of us. Was Mom going to leave

us in the lurch, now when our marks were so bad? It was shocking.

"The bus is here!" cried Julian, jumping from his chair.

"Maddie! Alexander! Quick, hurry!"

Dad practically threw us out the door. I think he was in a hurry to talk to Mom. He didn't seem too happy that she was going back to school.

On the school bus, I complained to my friends.

"No more fun and games, if my mom goes back to school."

"Not so!" Tough guy Patrick tried to cheer me up. "She'll have less time to get on your case."

"That'll just leave more room for my dad."

Then Little Miss Perfect Clementine

had to add her bossy two cents' worth.

"You really do have to study, Maddie."

"No, I don't, if I'm going to be a singer."

"Same for me," said Nicholas. "I'm going to inherit the family store."

"Then you'd better learn to add at least," sneered Patrick.

"Ever hear of a calculator, Smart Man?"

"You'd look pretty stupid if it broke down," said Clementine. "You really need to finish school if you want to get ahead."

Nicholas knew how to shut her up.

"You are so out of it, Clementine. These days, you can buy anything. To get ahead, you need to know how to bargain for what you want. And I don't need anybody to show me how to bargain."

Wow, I was impressed. You could tell Nicholas knew what he was talking about. I asked him if he knew a way I could bargain with my father.

"Just do what you have to — make promises, tell lies…"

"I was going to hide my report card from them," I said.

Clementine was shocked, but Patrick was curious. Nicholas went on explaining how to bargain.

It was really interesting!

2
Maddie Starts Bargaining

It was the last period. Ms. Spiegel's lips were moving, but I didn't hear what she was saying. I was reviewing Nicholas's notes. Finally the bell rang! I hurriedly gathered my things up.

"Maddie! You're forgetting your math assignment," Clementine reminded me. "It's due tomorrow."

She is such a pain! Who does she think she is — my mother? All of a sudden, I wondered if Mom would be at home when I got there. My uncertainty grew as the bus got closer to our house.

I think Alexander and Julian were wondering the same thing. They didn't run to the door when we got off the bus, but just followed me slowly in silence.

I opened the door. No sign of life. A heavy weight seemed to fall onto my shoulders. I was the oldest, so now I had to be responsible for my brothers. Grrr! I took them into the kitchen to get a snack.

"Hi, kids!"

Mom was there! Alexander and Julian threw themselves into her arms, as if she had just come back from a trip to the moon. I held back. I was mad. How could she have given me such a scare?

She finally noticed I was angry and

realized she had done something wrong.

"I'm sorry," she said. "I should have explained this morning how things would work, so you wouldn't worry."

She had arranged her schedule so that she would be home before we got back from school. Otherwise, Gran would be there, because she was going to look after Angelbaby.

"I even had time to bake a pie!" my mother exclaimed joyfully.

"I don't want any," I said. "I have to study."

And I turned my back and walked out. If she thinks she can butter me up by baking a pie …! Exactly! My mother was trying to buy me off! Incredible! Nicholas was right. You can buy anything. You just need to know

how to bargain.

I stretched out on my bed to think things over.

If I stayed mad, my mom would be nice to me. And Gran can never say no. As for my dad, I knew how to bargain with him. First I would have to show him that I was responsible....

At dinner, I brought a book down and pretended to study as I ate.

"That's not the right way to study," Julian started up again.

I felt like strangling the little genius. I figured his comment would set off an avalanche of reactions.

But no. Nobody said anything. The meal went on calmly, as if we had all gone through a frightening experience. I snuck a peek at my watch. Only five minutes until *Road to Stardom* came on.

I slipped out of the kitchen and went downstairs, hoping my father wouldn't.... Grrr, I could already hear him clumping down the stairs like a dinosaur.

"What did I tell you, Maddie?"

"That I need to work harder," I said innocently. "And I've already started, Dad! I'm going to get better marks. For sure!"

"We'll see when the next report card comes. In the meantime, you can forget about this program. Understand?"

"That's unfair!" I cried dramatically. "If my marks improve, I will have been punished unnecessarily for weeks!"

My father stood there with his mouth hanging open, looking confused.

Then he recovered. But he had to get the last word in.

"The first bad mark, then, and no more show."

He went back upstairs. How about that? I had figured out how to bargain with my father!

I happily watched my show, but a terrible thought hit me as I turned off

the TV. My math assignment! I had forgotten all about it. I was too tired now. I knew I would get a lousy mark on it.

Only Clementine could save me!

I called her up and began telling her a pack of lies. She agreed to give me a copy of her answers. I was amazed at how good I had become at bargaining.

A few days later, I saw how well it worked. My mark on the math

assignment was the best in the class. And I had never had more free time.

In the evening after dinner, my mother went upstairs to study. My dad had to clean up in the kitchen and take care of Angelbaby. He was too exhausted to bug me.

Gran took pity on him. Sometimes she would stay on to help him out. That gave me someone to talk to. She really listened when I told her about my career plans.

"A singer, Maddie?" she exclaimed. "That's not an easy job. Success is never guaranteed."

"Things have changed, Gran! All I have to do is win a contest. Then you become a star right away."

Gran was not convinced. I told her

I would give her a demonstration of my talent. She thought that was funny and suggested we invite the rest of the family.

"They need something to cheer them up," she said.

Mom said no, because she had a test the next day. But everyone else trooped downstairs to watch *Road to Stardom*. Even my dad. Unbelievable.

I put on quite a show for them. I sang and danced along with all the contestants. Angelbaby went wild. She shook her bottom and screamed at the top of her lungs. The others all clapped their hands. It was a fabulous party.

Which suddenly ended when my mother burst into the room like a volcano erupting.

"Will you please stop this racket? I can hear you from all the way upstairs. And it's Angelbaby's bedtime," she told my dad.

Then she stormed out.

My dad sighed and picked up Angelbaby. He was beginning to understand that going to school is not always great for everybody.

3
Math Test

I wasn't really paying attention the next day in class. After my triumphs the day before, I had no more worries for the future. I could already see —

Oops! Ms. Spiegel, standing in front of my desk.

"Class is over, Maddie. Are you staying behind to study?"

Very funny. Then she changed her tune and started lecturing me about how lazy I was, how I didn't pay attention, blah blah blah.

" … try to do better before the meeting with your parents. You'll have a chance to show that tomorrow."

I nodded mechanically. But I didn't remember anything special happening the next day.

When I got on the school bus, I asked my friends about it. Clementine was flabbergasted. She squeaked at me like a frightened mouse.

"Maddie, don't you remember? Tomorrow is the big term test in math!"

It was like an electric shock! If I failed that exam, I would fail the whole year in math. Nicholas looked terrified, too. His face turned whiter than a sheet of paper.

"There's no way you can review everything in one evening," Patrick added helpfully. "I started last night and I'm already about to go under."

Clementine had no mercy.

"I planned on four days of study and I made summaries of everything. All I have to do is review them this evening."

Nicholas and I stared at her like birds of prey. Either she didn't get our message, or she was playing dumb.

I gave her the final demand.

"You're our friend, right? And you want to stay friends, right? So give us your notes for review."

The little mouse was caught in the trap.

"Uh, sure, okay. But everything's at my house."

"Ever heard of email?" asked Nicholas. He didn't look so pale now.

"I have a great plan for how to use Clementine's stuff," he whispered in my ear. "And a ton of candy in my backpack. Interested?"

Yum! Of course I was interested. And after seeing his skills in bargaining, I thought I could trust him. I invited him to my house.

I told the family not to bother us and

dragged Nicholas down to the basement.
This time I was serious. I was really
going to study.

Nicholas immediately opened a bag
of chips. I took a handful and turned on
the computer. While we were waiting
for Clementine's email, he explained

his infallible plan to me.

"It's simple. We just have to cheat."

I practically choked.

"That's your plan? No way! It's too risky!"

"It's not risky at all. I've already done it," he announced.

I couldn't believe it! And I have to admit I was impressed. Nicholas wasn't as dumb as he looked. He had carried out this plan in secret, like a spy. He was fearless.

"It'll be a snap with Clementine's notes. We won't even have to copy anything out."

Ding! There was Clementine's email. Three pages of notes in perfect Clementine style. Everything was there, complete and ready to use. It was very tempting. I would be sure to pass.

Nicholas nudged me. "So, are you in?"

I decided I was in. And suddenly, I had a great idea.

"If we reduce the font size, we can fit it all on one page."

"Brilliant!" exclaimed Nicholas.

His enthusiasm spurred me on. I was bubbling with good ideas.

"We'll print one normal copy and cut it into separate summaries. Then we'll pick the ones that we have problems with."

Since we had problems with a lot of things, we wound up with a lot of summaries. I divided the pile in half.

"It'll be easy to trade them if we sit next to each other."

We rolled the papers up tightly and

managed to stuff them into our pens. Cheating sure was a lot of work. I was exhausted when we were finished.

Nicholas was riding high. It must be because he was used to doing it.

"This is great!" he said enthusiastically. "I'm glad I decided to do it with you."

That was pretty high praise, coming from Nicholas. And it's true that I came up with some good ideas. But once he had left, I began to have doubts. I started to feel sick. It was as if I didn't really want to cheat.

Maybe if I just studied a bit, I wouldn't have to ….

4
Maddie's Meltdown

Ms. Spiegel was handing out copies of the exam. The closer she got to my desk, the closer my nerves seemed to snapping.

Plop! The exam landed on my desk like a bomb. I held my breath as I read through it quickly. Then the bomb exploded, and everything went flying around in my head, quotients and divisors and denominators all mixed up.

I snuck a glance at Nicholas. He had lined his pens up in a row on his desk, and now he unhesitatingly selected one of them.

I turned back to my test paper.
I tried to concentrate on the first
question. How many 50 mL bottles
would it take to fill a 1 L bottle? That's
easy: two. No, maybe that's not right.
I moved on to the next question.
I couldn't understand a word of it,
so I went back to the mL thing.

I zipped open my pencil case.
My pens were in a bundle, held
together with an elastic. I tried to

remember which pen had the summary of the metric system. Right! The red one. I pulled it out. It was like there was a microphone in my pencil case, it made so much noise.

I heard someone sighing impatiently. Nicholas! What was he doing? I nudged him with my knee. He sighed again. I realized that he was not going to be any help. Now what would I do?

I squirmed in my seat. Only one thought seemed to flash through my brain: I was going to flunk the exam. Nooooo!

With sweaty hands I unscrewed the pen. I dropped the rolls of paper and they fell under my desk. I bent down to pick them up and there ... I saw Ms. Spiegel's feet. My heart stopped beating.

"Maddie, if you need to go to the washroom, you have only to ask."

"Uh, yes, may I please go to the washroom, Ms. Spiegel?"

I hurried out of the classroom on a wave of hope. In my pocket was the page with all of Clementine's summaries on it.

I locked myself in a stall and unfolded the sheet of paper.

All I could see was a big black splotch. Thousands of tiny little symbols. They jumped and wriggled about as the paper shook in my trembling hands. I opened my eyes wide and found my mLs. Millilitres: one thousand in a litre. Fifty goes more than two times into a thousand. Twenty times, then. But I was getting more and more tense.

I couldn't stay too long in the washroom. It would look suspicious. I was terrified. I scanned the paper looking for another answer. L equals fifty in Roman numerals. I threw the paper into the toilet and flushed it. Immediately, I wished I had it back. But it was too late. I had to go back to the classroom.

I made my way back to my seat, trembling from head to foot. I wrote the answer in about the mLs. Two 50 mL bottles to fill a 1 L bottle. Add CCXIX and LXVII. Let's see — that's 219 plus fifty — no, *sixty*-seven. That makes 286: CC...I couldn't think straight. I just filled in the answers sloppily. As soon as the bell rang, I leapt from my desk and ran past a startled

Ms. Spiegel. If I could only make it to the toilet in time … Whew.

As I flushed, I had another jolt. My sheet was still there, floating in the water. I fished it out and rolled it up into a ball and finally managed to flush it down.

I was destroyed, utterly destroyed. Pulverized.

As I climbed onto the school bus, I saw my friends laughing together. Even Nicholas! I suddenly became unpulverized and threw myself at him and chewed him out.

"I wasn't about to answer with The Eagle bearing down on us!" he said. "And anyway, I decided not to cheat. I figured it was too risky."

Then he told me that he had actually

never cheated before. He had lied to me to get me to go along with his plan. He knew I would figure out how to do it right.

"Just offer you a few chips, and you're eating out of my hand!"

That was shocking! Nicholas had tried to buy me! And he succeeded! That was really the icing on the cake, the whipped cream on a really great day. And Clementine added the cherry.

"I'm disgusted with you. I lent you my notes and you used them to cheat! Don't count on me to help you ever again!"

"Could be worse," Patrick said, trying to cheer me up. "Spiegel could have caught you."

Somehow I didn't feel any better. Instead, his words seemed to bring back the feelings I had had during the test. My fear washed over me again, and I felt sick.

As I stepped off the bus, I couldn't hold it back any longer. I threw up —

everything. It all came out: my fear, the test, Nicholas, the 1-litre bottle, the ball of paper, the cherry on the cake.

5
Consequences

I didn't want to draw attention to myself and what a wreck I was. That would only mean questions to answer. I walked through the kitchen without looking at anyone.

"I'm going upstairs to study!"

My mom was amazed. "You have all weekend to study, Maddie!"

I heard Gran say, "And she'll need it, with all the work she has to do!"

Poor Gran. She is the only one gullible enough to believe what I tell her.

I collapsed onto my bed and sank like a pita bread. I was flattened. I had

hardly enough time to take a breath before Gran burst into my room.
I had never seen her in such a state. She looked like a pit bull!

"Ms. Spiegel called," she said curtly.

That was all. Then silence.
The longer it lasted, the crazier I got.
Finally I cried desperately: "Everything she told you is a lie!"

Gran still had her pit bull look. It was too awful. I burst into tears. She didn't soften.

"What about the rolls of paper she found under your desk? Are those a lie?"

I had forgotten all about them!
It was all over, my life was ruined.
Still, I made an attempt to defend myself.

"Nicholas made me do it!"

"Nicholas will have the punishment he deserves," Gran replied. "And so will you. You reap what you sow, Maddie."

I felt like I was in an elevator hurtling down, down, down at top speed. I was about to crash when I managed to make out some of Gran's words.

" … write the exam over on Monday. I managed to persuade Ms. Spiegel to let you do that."

I kept on sobbing, but I felt a ray of hope. And it seemed to me that Gran's voice was not as angry as before.

"I didn't mention this to your parents. They have enough to worry about right now. You will have to tell them yourself, when this is all settled."

I swallowed hard and agreed.

I would do anything to wake up from this nightmare.

"I told your parents that I was inviting you over for the weekend."

That sounded great to me. I would have perfect conditions for studying. There would be no distractions, no one to bug me.

But when I got to Gran's house, I had a rude awakening. She had drawn up a whole study program for me. And she was the strictest teacher I had ever had. No mistakes allowed! You did it over and over until you got it right.

But it worked! It is absolutely amazing what you can learn if you study.

And I began to enjoy it. Every right answer was like a victory. And Gran

loved every second of it. She wasn't
like a pit bull anymore. She called me
her dearest little denominator!

***

I breezed through the exam. A piece of
cake! And I got the top mark in the class.

Clementine found this a little hard to
swallow.

"When I think where you started from, it's like a miracle!"

"I have my own study methods," I told her. "You should be happy. I won't have to borrow your notes anymore."

Take that, Little Miss Perfect!

Nicholas found it even harder to take, because he flunked his exam.

"You cheated, but you were allowed to write the test again. That's not fair."

But I had seen that coming, and I had my answer all ready.

"I can go and tell them you cheated, too, if you like."

He turned pale. And then, you'll never guess what he did. He offered me a bag of chips.

He must think I'm an idiot.
He really needed to be taught a lesson.

I took the bag of chips, just as I would if he had bought me off. I opened it up and poured the chips on the ground. Wow! Did that ever feel good! And I was proud of myself, because I really wanted to eat those chips.

***

I have never been so eager to show off one of my tests. Ms. Spiegel had stuck stars all over it.

At the dinner table, I laid the test on

my dad's plate. His face lit up.

"I am dazzled, Maddie! But I knew you could do it. I was right to trust in you."

Yikes. He must never, never find out that I cheated. At least not yet. I would hate to spoil his pleasure. Honestly!

We ate our dinner in peace and harmony. Then my brother Julian had to ruin it all. As we were leaving the table, he piped up.

"Don't forget, tomorrow is parents' night at school."

"You've got to come," Alexander insisted. "For once, my teacher has nothing to complain about."

The same couldn't be said of Ms. Spiegel! I looked imploringly at Gran. She just stared back, and I could see a pit bull gleam in her eyes. I would not be able to escape my fate. So I lowered my head and told my parents everything.

Afterwards, there was silence, as heavy as a ton of bricks. I felt like all those bricks were about to land on my head.

But to my amazement, my dad said only, "I think you have probably learned a lot from this experience."

Obviously, I had to agree. I repeated

Gran's fine words about working hard, and reaping what I had sown, and so on and so forth. And I promised I would never cheat again.

"I was too scared!"

My dad cracked up. My mom, on the other hand, did not think it was funny at all. Instead, she unloaded the ton of bricks on me. The last brick was the worst of all.

" ... brought shame on your family. It was very wrong of Gran not to tell us what you had done. It makes us look like parents who — "

"How soon you forget!" Gran interrupted.

My mom was stunned. And she never recovered, because Gran went on to tell us some fine stories about her.

When she was young, my mom never did a lick of work. She only wanted to go out and have fun. She dreamed of becoming a movie star.

My dad started teasing her. He said she was like the grasshopper in the fable.

"The grasshopper all summer long
Sang her song ..."

And he burst out laughing. Gran laughed, too, and so did my mom. But not like she thought it was funny. That was another lesson for me. I hope I won't still have to go to school when I'm as old as my mom! As I looked at my exam paper, I realized that stars don't just fall out of the sky. Only in my dreams…

More new novels in the *First Novels Series*!

Toby Laughs Last
Jean Lemieux
Illustrated by Sophie Casson
Translated by Sarah Cummins

When Toby climbs too high in a tree to rescue a kite, he tumbles to the ground and has to go to hospital. The doctors stick tubes down his throat and bandage him up. Toby is happy to be alive — but then he realizes that he can't laugh any more. Toby wonders: what part of your body does laughter come from? And what can he do to get his laughter back?

In this story, Toby finds out just how important it is to be able to laugh.

Toni Biscotti's Magic Trick
Caroline Merola
Illustrated by Caroline Merola
Translated by Sarah Cummins

Toni Biscotti is shy — really shy. Yet for some reason she has signed up to perform at the school concert. Will she be able to put together an act good enough to impress Marco Pirelli? Toni can't dance, can't sing, can't play a musical instrument — what on earth is she going to do? Perhaps her grandmother the sorcerer can help her out…

In this story, Toni discovers that it's not really so hard to make magic happen.

Super Move, Morgan
Ted Staunton
Illustrated by Bill Slavin

Morgan accuses Aldeen Hummel, the Godzilla of Grade Three, of taking his Commander Crunch action figure. But did she really take it, or has Morgan just made another "super" move?

In this story, Morgan learns a lesson about honesty and judging others.

Lilly Takes the Lead
Brenda Bellingham
Illustrated by Clarke MacDonald

Lilly and her friends argue one lunchtime over eating good and bad foods. They talk about fat people and skinny people, and Lilly wonders why people think that fat people can't be healthy and beautiful. Then when the kids are at track and field practice there is an emergency, and Lilly and Theresa take charge.

In this story, Lilly learns that what matters most is how people are on the inside.

Formac Publishing Company Limited
5502 Atlantic Street
Halifax, Nova Scotia B3H 1G4

Orders: 1-800-565-1975
Fax: 902-425-0166
www.formac.ca